Written by
James Gelsey

WORLDWIDE PUBLISHING
WB
TM

A
LITTLE APPLE
PAPERBACK

SCHOLASTIC INC.

New York   Toronto   London   Auckland   Sydney
Mexico City   New Delhi   Hong Kong   Buenos Aires

For Ms. Case's 2000-2001
3rd grade class,
Tenafly, NJ

ISBN 0-439-28486-4

SCOOBY-DOO and all related characters and elements
are trademarks of and © Hanna-Barbera.
CARTOON NETWORK and logo are trademarks of
and © Cartoon Network.
(s02)
Published by Scholastic Inc. All rights reserved.
SCHOLASTIC, LITTLE APPLE PAPERBACKS, and associated logos are trademarks and/or registered trademarks of Scholastic Inc.

Designed by Carisa Swenson

12 11 10 9 8 7 6 5 4 3 2 1   2 3 4 5 6 7/0

Special thanks to Duendes del Sur for cover and interior illustrations.
Printed in the U.S.A.
First Scholastic printing, February 2002

Chapter 1

The Mystery Machine cruised down the highway, heading for Happy Sally Land, a brand-new amusement park just outside of town. Suddenly, a strange popping sound came from the back of the van.

"Jinkies!" Velma exclaimed. "That sounds like a flat tire."

"I hope not," Daphne said. "I don't want to be late getting to Happy Sally Land."

"I'll check it out," Fred said, carefully slowing the van to a stop. He got out and went to take a look. A moment later, Fred hopped back into the van and started the engine.

"No flat," he reported. "And nothing seems to be wrong with the muffler, either. We must have run over something lying on the road."

He steered the van onto the highway, and the gang was back on their way. A moment later, however, they heard the popping sound again. But this time there was another sound, too.

"Ree-hee-hee-hee-hee-hee-hee-hee," giggled Scooby.

Daphne and Velma turned around.

"What are you two doing back there?" Daphne asked.

Shaggy looked up with something green hanging out of his mouth.

"Like, shorry, guysh," Shaggy said. He spit out the green thing. "Scoob and I saw a picture of people carrying balloon animals and decided to try to make them ourselves. But every time I try to bend the balloons, they pop."

"Oh, brother," Velma said, rolling her eyes. "Shaggy, you have to use special balloons for making animals and things."

"Velma's right," Daphne continued. "You need the long, skinny balloons. Besides, where'd you see a picture of people carrying balloon animals?"

"Rere," Scooby said, handing Daphne a brochure. She unfolded it and looked at all the pictures.

"I don't see anyone carrying a balloon animal," she said.

"Like, it's right there, Daph," Shaggy said, pointing. "The little kid."

Daphne squinted her eyes and examined

the picture more closely. Sure enough, in the upper right-hand corner was a little girl holding a dog made out of a balloon.

"Is that really what you're looking forward to about our visit to Happy Sally Land?" called Fred from the front seat. "Daphne's uncle didn't get us VIP passes to the pre-Grand Opening just so we could get balloon animals."

"That's right," Daphne said. "We're going to help test out the new rides, like the Nordic Nor'easter."

"That sounds like a really cold rainstorm to me," joked Shaggy.

"Actually, it's the largest roller coaster around," Velma said.

"Roller roaster?" Scooby barked. A big smile spread across his face.

"Like, we love roller coasters!" Shaggy exclaimed.

"You know that we're talking about a roller *coaster* and not a roller *skate*, right?" Velma said. "The Nordic Nor'easter is supposed to be the biggest and fastest roller coaster there is."

"Not to mention the scariest," Fred added.

"Man, there isn't a roller coaster big enough or fast enough to scare me and Scooby," Shaggy replied. "Right, Scoob?"

"Right," barked Scooby.

Fred, Daphne, and Velma glanced at one another. Then Daphne turned back to Shaggy and Scooby.

"Well, then, you'll have a chance to be one of the first to experience the Nordic Nor'easter," she said. "Unless you get sidetracked by all those balloon animals."

"Speaking of balloons," Fred said, pointing to the windshield, "check those out."

In the distance, the gang could see hundreds of balloons flying through the sky.

"We must be getting close to Happy Sally Land," Velma noted. "This is probably part of the welcome."

"That's a great welcome, all right," Daphne agreed. "But I'm surprised they'd let one of their big character balloons go."

Sure enough, an enormous balloon in the shape of a Viking was floating in the air behind the others. But there was something hanging off the side of the balloon.

"Like, it looks like that Viking's losing his belt," Shaggy said.

"That's a banner, not a belt," Velma said. "It's probably a welcome banner."

"If it is, it's the strangest welcome I've ever seen," Daphne said.

"Why? What does it say?" Fred asked.

"Beware!" said Daphne.

Chapter 2

A few minutes later, Fred steered the Mystery Machine into the Happy Sally Land parking lot. The gang got out of the van and made their way through the main gates. A short woman was greeting guests by handing out headbands with yellow antennas attached. The woman had long blond hair and was wearing one of the antennas on top of her head. As the gang got closer, they saw a tiny yellow smiley face bobbing around at the end of a long, curly wire. The woman saw Daphne and ran over.

"Daphne!" the woman yelled cheerfully. "It's great to see you!" She gave Daphne a big hug.

"Hello, Sally," Daphne replied. "It's wonderful to see you, too. These are my friends. This is Fred, Velma, Shaggy, and Scooby-Doo. Shaggy and Scooby are very excited about riding the Nordic Nor'easter."

"Well, that's just stupendous!" Sally declared. "Welcome to Happy Sally Land, all. Here, have a Happy Bippy." She handed everyone their own antenna.

"Thanks, Sally," Daphne said, putting the antenna on her head. Fred and Velma followed Daphne's example.

"Well, Shaggy and Scooby, aren't you going to put yours on?" asked Velma.

"Like, we'd love to, but we just washed our hair this morning and we can't do a thing with it," Shaggy replied.

"That's okay," Sally said. "Not everyone

gets into the spirit of Happy Sally Land right away. Oh, did I mention that all of the snack bars have been instructed to give free food to anyone wearing a Happy Bippy today?"

"Ree rood?" barked Scooby. "Rhy ridn't rou ray ro?" Scooby snatched his Happy Bippy from Shaggy and plopped it on top of his head. Shaggy did the same.

"I sure feel silly," he said. "But I'd rather feel silly than hungry any day. Now, which way to the food?"

"Not so fast, Shaggy," Fred said. "We want to ask Sally something first."

"What is it?" asked Sally.

"On our way over, we noticed a giant Viking balloon with a banner that read 'Beware,'" Velma said.

Sally's shoulders drooped and her smile melted into a small frown.

"I was hoping no one would notice," she sighed.

"Like, it's hard to miss a ten-story-tall Viking floating through the sky," Shaggy joked. Daphne gave him a stern look.

"We were practicing our Happy Sally Land Festival of Balloons Parade," Sally explained. "We have giant balloons that represent different areas of the park. Somehow, someone attached that warning to the Viking balloon and managed to release it. Someone's trying to scare people away from the park, and I have no idea who it could be."

"It's probably someone who doesn't want the park to open," a voice said from behind them.

The gang turned around and saw a giant daisy standing there.

"Rikes! A riant ralking raisy!" Scooby

gasped, jumping into Shaggy's arms.

"Relax, Scooby," Daphne said. "It's just one of the park employees dressed up like a big daisy."

"This is my nephew, Gary Goosage," Sally said. "Isn't he adorable?"

Gary rolled his eyes. "I told you, Aunt Sally, I hate being dressed like a daisy!" he complained. "Why couldn't you let me be in charge of the Nordic Nor'easter? I've spent all my spare time learning how to operate it. Look, I even drew a picture and took notes."

Gary reached inside the stem part of his costume and took out a creased piece of paper.

"I'm really proud of you for trying so hard, Gary," Sally said, smiling fondly at her nephew. "But you know my policy: no favors for family. Now I have to run along to the Nordic Nor'easter and make sure everything's ready. Daphne, I'll see you and your friends there soon, okay?"

"Okay. See you later, Sally!" Daphne replied. Happy Sally walked away, handing out Happy Bippys to anyone not wearing one.

"The least she could do is give me a chance," Gary complained to the gang. "But no, I have to spend my days dressed like a stupid flower. I wish there was some way I could change her mind." Gary looked up and saw a red rose, purple tulip, and yellow daffodil walking toward him. "Anyway, I gotta go. The rest of my bouquet is here. Have a Happy Sally Land kind of day." Gary walked over to join the other flowers, and they all disappeared into the crowd.

"Well, gang, what do you say we explore Happy Sally Land?" asked Fred.

"To the rides!" exclaimed Daphne.

"To the food!" shouted Shaggy.

Chapter 3

The gang followed the main path to the center of Happy Sally Land. There they found an enormous fountain three stories tall. It had sculptures of flying dolphins, dancing elephants, and marching flamingos. Water spurted out everywhere and collected in the oversize pool at the base.

"What a groovy fountain," Daphne said. "Don't you think so, Velma?"

Everyone looked up and admired the fountain. Shaggy took a glance and noticed one of the flamingos.

"Hey, I think that flamingo just winked at me!" he shouted.

"Shaggy, it's a fountain," Velma said. "It's made out of stone or cement or a polyurethane-based resin. It can't wink."

"Sure I can," the flamingo said. "I can talk, too!"

"Zoinks!" Shaggy exclaimed. "It's a haunted fountain!"

"A magic fountain is more like it," the flamingo retorted. "After all, this is Happy Sally Land." Then the flamingo let out a loud *BUUURRRRPPP*!

"Ruh?" said Scooby, cocking his head at the flamingo.

"Sorry about that," the flamingo's voice said. Only now, the voice sounded like it was coming from behind them. Everyone turned and saw a man wearing a Happy Bippy. He wore a blue denim shirt and brown safari vest, and was holding a can of soda in one hand.

16

"I was testing out the fountain from back there," he said with a slight foreign accent. He held up a small rectangular box covered with knobs and switches.

"What's that?" asked Fred.

"It's a remote control unit for the fountain," the man explained. "These switches can make the animals wink, wiggle their ears, and spurt water. I used this built-in microphone to talk to you. I'm trying to convince Sally to put these out for the guests to use."

"Did you design the fountain?" Velma asked.

"As a matter of fact, I did," the man said. "I'm Sasha Kashikova, a specialist at merging creativity and engineering."

"Jinkies! Did you design anything else in the park?" Velma inquired.

Sasha's obvious pride quickly faded away as he lowered the arm holding the remote control unit.

"Yes, but it is too painful to discuss," Sasha replied melodramatically.

"In that case, do you, like, know where the closest snack bar is?" asked Shaggy.

"Don't bother. The food here is as terrible as the rides," Sasha announced. "Besides, the fountain is the only thing here worth seeing."

"What about the Nordic Nor'easter?" asked Fred.

"To be honest, I get sick whenever I ride roller coasters," Sasha said. "But that doesn't stop me from designing them."

"Did you design the Nordic Nor'easter, Mr. Kashikova?" guessed Daphne.

Sasha's face clouded with disappointment. "I told you, it is too painful to discuss,"

18

he said. The gang looked at one another and shrugged.

"Well, it was nice meet —" began Fred.

"But if you insist, I will tell you," Sasha interrupted. "After I designed the fountain, Sally asked me to submit a design for a new roller coaster. So I sent her a drawing of my idea. Look."

He took out his wallet and removed a tiny square of paper. He unfolded it once, twice, three times, four times, until it was the size of an envelope. Then he opened the envelope

and took out another tattered piece of paper. He unfolded it until it was as large as a pizza box.

"This is the roller-coaster design I sent her. I called it the Norwegian Blizzard," Sasha said. The gang looked at the paper and saw a sketch of a roller coaster. "But she never even looked it at. She simply sent it back to me un-opened. Imagine my surprise when I came to work on the fountain and saw the Nordic Nor'easter. I realized then that Sally must have somehow stolen my idea for the roller coaster!"

"Did you ever say anything to her?" asked Fred.

"Who can say anything to her?" Sasha shouted angrily. "Happy Sally's so . . . so . . . so . . ."

"Happy?" suggested Shaggy.

"Yes, happy!" Sasha bellowed. "She's just so happy all the time that it's impossible to be angry at her! And I am *so* angry at her!"

Sasha Kashikova turned and stormed away.

"Jeepers, it's hard to see how someone so angry could make a fountain that's so whimsical and fun," Daphne said.

"The only kind of fountain Scooby and I are interested in right now is a soda fountain," Shaggy said. "Come on, Scoob. Let's shake our Happy Bippys and find some free food."

Chapter 4

After downing a few orders of free french fries at Happy Sally's Spectacular Spuds, the gang followed signs for the Nordic Nor'easter. The path led them through a trail of dense foliage. When they came out, they found themselves standing in the Viking Village. In the middle of the village clearing stood a replica of a Viking ship with a large, square sail. The head of the ship was shaped like a fierce dragon. A row of long oars hung off each side of the ship.

Three Viking homes stood in a line to one

side of the ship. They were built from timber planks and had thatched roofs. On the opposite side there was a long house built from stone. Statues of Viking warriors dressed in long furs and holding swords were lined up around the village. A few statues of Viking villagers engaged in different everyday chores were posed throughout the village.

But Shaggy and Scooby weren't looking at the Viking Village. Their attention was focused on what they saw in the distance behind the Viking ship. It was the Nordic Nor'easter, the largest roller coaster they had ever seen. An enormous picture of a fierce Viking wearing an iron helmet and holding a battle-ax and an iron shield covered the side of the roller coaster's first hill. The coaster itself towered over the trees and made the Viking Village look like a toy set.

"Gulp," Shaggy said, the color slowly draining from his face.

"What's the matter, Shaggy?" asked Daphne. "I thought you said there was no roller coaster big enough to scare you and Scooby."

"Sc-sc-scared? Who said anything about being scared?" said Shaggy. "I'm, uh, just, like, feeling a little sick from all those french fries."

"Re, roo," Scooby echoed, holding his stomach and pretending to be sick.

"Well, the whole thing makes me sick," said a woman next to them. She stood with her hands on her hips and a sour expression on her face. The only thing happy about her was the Happy Bippy bopping around on her head.

"Just look at how these Vikings are being portrayed," she said with exasperation. "They look like a bunch of backward, uneducated farmers. The truth is that the Viking people were very resourceful. But all people seem to care about are those metal helmets with the horns sticking out. It's enough to make you sick, all right."

The woman looked over at the gang and saw their surprised looks.

"I'm sorry," the woman apologized. "I always get worked up about this stuff. My name is Lena. Lena Furswich."

"It's nice to meet you, Ms. Furswich," Velma said. "You seem to know an awful lot about the Vikings."

"That's because I am descended from a Viking family," Lena explained. "I hoped that Happy Sally would use this opportunity to teach people about Viking culture. But instead she chose to exploit it and continue unpleasant stereotypes. Someone needs to send her a message that this is just not acceptable!

I'm sorry, you'll have to excuse me. I can't stay here another minute."

Lena quickly walked around the side of the Viking ship and disappeared.

"If we're going to meet Sally, we'd better get going," Fred announced.

The gang followed the path Lena had taken around the Viking ship and found a path on the other side. More statues of Vikings in full warrior gear lined the path. Some of the Vikings held shields and swords. Some held spears and some held battle-axes.

"Man, these Vikings sure give me the creeps," Daphne said.

"Oh, there you are!" called Happy Sally from the end of the path. "Have I got a surprise for you!"

"What is it?" asked Fred.

"Since Shaggy and Scooby seemed so eager to ride the roller coaster, I have decided to let them be the very first guests to ride the

Nordic Nor'easter," Sally announced. "What do you have to say about that?"

Shaggy and Scooby looked at each other and held their stomachs.

"Us and our big mouths!" moaned Shaggy.

Chapter 5

A crowd had gathered beneath the canopy in front of the Nordic Nor'easter. The gang could see the empty roller-coaster car sitting in the station immediately behind the canopy. The roller-coaster car looked like a Viking ship but was really made up of eight individual cars hooked together. The tracks led straight out of the station, curved to the right, and then went up an enormous hill.

Happy Sally elbowed her way through the crowd and stood on a short platform right in front of the entrance to the roller coaster.

"Good afternoon, friends," she called. "And welcome to Happy Sally Land!"

Everyone burst into applause.

"Thank you all so much for coming," Sally continued. "I am so excited about today, I could just burst into a thousand pieces of confetti right now! I am proud to introduce to you the largest roller coaster around. It's fully computerized and has been programmed to provide the ultimate thrill experience. Ladies and gentlemen, I proudly present the Nordic Nor'easter!"

Everyone clapped and cheered again.

"And now, to take the inaugural ride . . ." Sally began to announce.

"Oh, no," moaned Shaggy. "That's us. Quick, Scooby, pretend to be invisible. Maybe she won't see us."

". . . I could think of no one more fitting," Sally continued, "than the Happy Sally Land official mascot, Mr. Happy Bippy!"

The giant tulip and rose that the gang had seen before walked over to Sally holding a smiley-face doll as big as Sally herself.

"Follow me, everyone," Sally called. She took the giant doll and walked through the turnstile. Then she put Mr. Happy Bippy into the front seat of the roller-coaster car and put down the safety harness. Next, she took a black rectangular box out of her pocket.

"I will now launch the Nordic Nor'easter by remote control," she announced. "Everyone count down with me. Five!"

"Four! Three! Two!" shouted the crowd. "ONE!"

Sally pushed a button on the box. The Viking ship lurched forward, stopped, then began again, taking off down the track.

Just as everyone turned to watch the Viking ship begin its ascent, they heard a loud howl come from behind them.

"BEEEEE-WAAAAAAARE THE VIKING!"

A fierce-looking man in Viking costume ran down the path. He had a long, bushy moustache and beard, and he was dressed just like one of the warrior Viking statues, complete with a long fur pelt, a shiny metal helmet with horns on it, and a mighty shield made of wood and iron. The Viking shoved his way through the crowd, jumped over the turnstile, and leaped over the roller-coaster track to the far side of the station.

"I warned you to beware of the Viking!" he shouted. "Maybe you need a display of my power to convince you to obey!" The Viking reached into his pelt with one hand and raised his sword high into the air with the other. He pointed the sword at the Viking ship as it continued up the hill.

"By the power of Asgard, I command you to stop!" he shouted.

The Viking ship roller-coaster car abruptly stopped in its tracks. Everyone gasped.

"Leave this park and never come back!" the Viking howled at the guests. "Leave, before I bring the rest of my Viking warriors back to life!"

The Viking let out another creepy-sounding howl and then ran off. There was so much commotion in the crowd that he disappeared easily. The guests started running away. Some even climbed through the bushes rather than go back through the Viking Village.

"Wait! Wait! Come back!" shouted Sally. But it was no use. Everyone but Fred,

Daphne, and Velma had cleared out. Sally turned and they could see a single tear trickle down her cheek.

"Don't worry, Sally, everything will be all right," Daphne said with a smile.

"An angry Viking's scared everyone away. My roller coaster is broken. My special day has been ruined. If word gets out, I may not even be able to open the park at all," Sally said sadly. Then she noticed that Daphne and the others were still smiling. "How can you all be happy at a time like this?" she asked.

"Because Mystery, Inc. is on the case!" the gang cheered together.

Chapter 6

"Sally, you take care of the guests, and we'll take care of the Viking," Daphne reassured her. "We'll get to the bottom of this mystery before you know it."

"Thank you, kids," Sally said, her smile starting to return. "I'll catch up with you later. No time to dawdle. So many smiles to restore on frowning faces." Sally ran up the path and started searching for her guests.

"Gang, let's take a quick look around the station here before we split up to look for clues," Fred suggested.

"Maybe we should start by looking for Shaggy and Scooby," Velma said. "They disappeared soon after the Viking showed up."

The three of them looked around. The station area was empty, except for a brown shoe.

"Where did this come from?" wondered Daphne, picking up the shoe. "Hey! It looks like Shaggy's."

THUD! Another shoe fell to the floor next to Daphne. Fred, Daphne, and Velma looked up and saw Shaggy and Scooby holding on to the metal frame beneath the canopy.

"Like, there was so much commotion, the only direction Scoob and I could go was up," Shaggy explained.

"Well, what goes up, must come down," Velma said.

"Right on, Velma," Shaggy called. "On three, Scoob. One. Two. Three!" Shaggy and Scooby dropped to the ground next to their friends. Daphne handed Shaggy his shoes.

"Thanks, Daph," he replied. "You okay, Scoob?"

"Rou ret!" barked Scooby.

"Now that we're done clowning around, it's time to look for clues," Fred said.

"Here you go, Scoob, you dropped your Happy Bippy," Shaggy said, handing Scooby a smiley-face antenna.

"Rat's rot mine," Scooby said, pointing to the bobbing antenna on his head.

"It's not mine," Shaggy said, taking his out of his pocket.

"We all have ours, too," Fred said, checking his head and glancing at Daphne and Velma.

"If it's not any of ours, then whose is it?" asked Shaggy.

"It must belong to the only other person who was over here," Velma concluded. "The Viking! He must have had it on under his helmet."

Shaggy dropped the Happy Bippy to the ground.

"I don't want to be around when he comes back looking for it," Shaggy announced. "Let's get out of here."

"Hold on, you two," Velma said. "We're not going anywhere until we solve this mystery."

"I was afraid you were going to say that," Shaggy moaned.

"I think the Viking ran off down the path behind

the station," Fred said. "Daphne and I will look around here some more, then check it out."

"And Shaggy, Scooby, and I will look around the Viking Village," Velma said. "I have a hunch that's where he was hiding before he showed up. Come on, Shaggy. Let's go, Scooby-Doo."

Shaggy and Scooby followed Velma up the path to the Viking Village. As they neared the village square, they saw the rows of Viking statues lining the path.

"Ruh-uh," Scooby said, stopping short. "Rot ris ray."

"They're just statues, Scooby," Velma said. She walked over to one and knocked on its chest.

"See? It's probably nothing but plastic and cement with a coat of paint on it. Now let's get going." Velma continued down the path.

"Velma's right, Scoob," Shaggy said.

"We've got nothing to worry about." Shaggy turned and started walking toward the village. Scooby walked right behind Shaggy and precisely followed his footsteps.

"Watch it, Scoob. If you were any closer, you'd be in front of me," Shaggy complained. "You've got nothing to worry about. See?" He walked over to one of the Viking statues and knocked on its chest like Velma had. But instead of a light, tapping sound, the knock gave off a heavy thump.

"Hmm, this statue's kind of soft," Shaggy noticed, poking around the statue's chest. "Must be a little soggy from the rain."

Scooby's eyes opened wide. "R-r-r-r-raggy!" he barked.

"What is it, Scoob?"

"RIKING!" Scooby shouted.

"Like, I know it's a Viking, Scooby," Shaggy said, looking at the statue. "It's just another Viking statue."

The statue's right arm moved slowly up into the air. "It's j-j-just another V-V-V-Viking statue that's moving its arms. ZOINKS! It's the Viking! Run, Scooby!"

Scooby took off down the path, with Shaggy close behind. The Viking statue jumped off its short pedestal and took off after them.

"Help! The Viking's after us!" Shaggy called.

Chapter 7

As Shaggy and Scooby ran down the path into the Viking Village, they could hear the Viking howling after them.

"Quick, Scoob, find someplace to hide!" Shaggy shouted.

They ran onto the Viking ship in the middle of the village and found an open chest on the deck. They tossed out a large net and other fishing tools and jumped inside, pulling the lid shut.

"I think we lost him, Scooby," Shaggy whispered.

Then they heard someone walk onto the ship. The footsteps got louder and heavier as they neared the treasure chest.

"He's found us!" Shaggy cried. "Quick, Scoob, close your eyes. Maybe if we can't see him, he won't be able to see us."

Shaggy and Scooby closed their eyes tight. They heard the creak of the lid as it opened.

"What are you two doing in there?" a familiar voice asked.

Shaggy and Scooby opened their eyes and saw a giant daisy. It was Gary Goosage.

"Have you seen, like, a runaway Viking around here?" asked Shaggy.

"No," the daisy replied. "You're not supposed to be in there, you know. It's against the rules."

"Sorry," Shaggy said as they climbed out.

"Not as sorry as I am about having to walk around dressed like this all day," Gary complained. "Anyway, I'm supposed to make sure all the guests who are still here are having fun. Are you having fun?"

"For me, there's nothing like solving a good mystery," Velma said, joining them on deck. "So I am still having fun."

"Great," Gary said without the slightest bit of enthusiasm. "My work here is done. Have a Happy Sally Land kind of day." Gary walked off the ship and down the path back to the center of the park.

"Now what are you two doing up here?" Velma asked. "We're supposed to be looking for clues."

"But the Viking chased us all the way down the path," Shaggy explained. "We thought he was one of the statues, but when

I went to show Scooby he was really made of plastic and cement like you did, the statue turned out to be made of arms and howls and stuff."

Scooby posed like the statue and then raised his arm like the statue had. Then he let out a howl and pretended to chase Shaggy around the ship.

"Just like that, Velma," Shaggy said, pointing to Scooby. "Velma? Velma?"

Velma wasn't listening. She was examining something on the ground that had caught her eye.

"Did you say he chased you down the path?" Velma asked, stepping off the boat. She walked over to the end of the path and knelt down to pick up a small piece of paper. She unfolded it and began to scrutinize it.

"Hmmm, this is interesting," she said.

"What is?" asked Fred and Daphne as they came down the path from the roller-coaster. "Did you find a clue?"

"I think so," Velma said, showing them the paper. "It looks like a piece of a drawing of some kind."

"That is interesting, Velma," Fred agreed.

"Almost as interesting as this," Daphne said. "Look."

She opened her hand to reveal a small black knob.

"Hey, that looks like the knob on Sally's remote control unit," Velma said.

"Except we found it on the path behind the roller-coaster station," Daphne explained. "Where the Viking was."

"I think it's time to send this Viking sailing out of Happy Sally Land," Velma said.

"Velma's right, gang," Fred said. "It's time to set a trap. And we need to act fast before everyone leaves the park, so listen up. Daphne, you go find Sally. Velma and I will hide behind the row of statues on the left side of the path. We'll get the fishing net from the Viking ship, and when the Viking runs by us, we'll toss the net over him."

"Sounds like a good plan to me," Shaggy said. "In fact, any plan in which I don't hear my name sounds like a good plan to me."

"Me, roo," echoed Scooby.

"Then I don't think you're going to like the plan after all," Fred said.

"I knew it was too good to be true," Shaggy sighed.

Chapter 8

"Don't worry, Shaggy, you and Scooby won't have to do much," Daphne said. "Just get the Viking to chase you."

"Is that all?" asked Shaggy. "Like, we've already been on that ride, thanks. And I think we've had about all the fun we can. So have a Happy Sally Land kind of day, everyone. Let's go, Scooby."

But before they could go anywhere, Fred grabbed the back of Shaggy's shirt. "Sorry, Shaggy, but we need your help," Fred said.

"What do you say, Scooby?" asked

Daphne. "Will you do it for a Scooby Snack?"

Scooby shook his head. "Ruh-uh."

"How about two Scooby Snacks?" asked Velma.

Scooby's eyes lit up.

"Rokay!" he barked. Daphne and Velma each tossed a Scooby Snack high into the air. Scooby jumped up and gobbled them down, his smiley-face antenna bobbing.

"Now let's get started," Fred said. "Velma, I'll get the net and then we can get into position behind the statues. Good luck, Shaggy and Scooby."

Fred grabbed the net from the Viking ship. Then he and Velma walked over to the row of statues by the path. Shaggy and Scooby stood in the middle of the Viking Village and looked around.

"I don't know about you, Scooby, but I could never be a Viking," Shaggy said. "Like, no electricity, no television."

"Ro rizza," Scooby added.

"Man, you said it, Scoob," Shaggy agreed. "What do you say we go back onto the ship and keep a lookout for you-know-who?"

They climbed onto the Viking ship and sat down on one of the rowing benches along the sides. The end of a long oar lay on the bench in front of them. Shaggy grabbed the oar and pretended to row.

"Row, row, row your boat, gently down the stream," sang Shaggy.

Scooby grabbed the oar and began rowing with Shaggy.

"Rerrily, rerrily, rerrily, rerrily, rife ris rut a ream," he sang.

"Great job, Scoob. Now let's do it in a round," Shaggy said. "I'll start. Row, row, row your boat, gently down —"

"Row, row, row your boat," another voice sang.

"Scooby, you started too early," Shaggy said.

"Rasn't me," Scooby said.

"Well, if it wasn't you, and it wasn't me, then who . . ."

"Merrily, merrily, merrily, merrily, life is but a dream," the voice sang.

Shaggy and Scooby looked at each other. Then they slowly turned around and saw the Viking!

"Zoinks!" shouted Shaggy. "This way, Scoob!"

Shaggy and Scooby jumped off the ship and headed for the path. The Viking howled as he got closer to them.

"Make way!" shouted Shaggy.

Fred and Velma peered out from behind the statues and saw the Viking approach. They jumped out and threw the net over him.

"Gotcha!" Velma shouted.

Shaggy and Scooby stopped running. The Viking fumbled under the net, trying to get free. Then he reached down and took out his sword. With a lightning-fast *swish*, the Viking had sliced through the net. He threw off the net and started after Shaggy and Scooby again. Shaggy dived out of the way, but Scooby kept running.

The Viking chased Scooby all the way down the path and back to the Nordic Nor'easter. Scooby jumped over the turnstile and ran straight for the roller-coaster car sitting in the station. He jumped into the front seat of the roller-coaster car and ducked down.

The Viking tried to jump over the turnstile, too, but tripped and fell to the ground. As he did, the roller-coaster car suddenly lurched forward. The Viking stood up and saw the roller-coaster car moving out of the station. He ran onto the platform and jumped into the last seat just as the car pulled away.

Scooby sat up and saw that he was moving.

"Relp! Raggy!" he called.

Fred, Velma, and Shaggy watched as the Viking stood up in the rear seat and started climbing toward the front of the car.

"The Viking's behind you!" Fred shouted.

"Behind you, Scooby!" Velma echoed.

Scooby was too far away to hear. The ship had already started climbing up the enormous first hill. The Viking climbed over the seats, getting closer to Scooby. Just as the ship reached the top of the hill, he jumped into the seat next to Scooby. They both looked down and realized they were at the top.

"AAAAAAAAAAAAAAAAAHHHHHHHH-HHHHHHH!" cried the Viking as the ship plummeted down the other side of the hill and took off along the tracks.

When the ship pulled back into the station, Scooby had a huge smile on his face.

"Scooby, are you all right?" asked Shaggy.

"Rou ret!" he barked.

"But where's the Viking?" asked Velma.

"Rere!" Scooby said. He pointed to the Viking, who was slumped on the floor of the car, sick as a dog.

Chapter 9

Happy Sally and Daphne ran into the station house.

"We looked for you in the village, but then we heard someone screaming on the roller coaster," Daphne said.

Sally watched as Shaggy and Fred helped the Viking out of the roller-coaster car.

"Well, Sally, would you like to see who's really been scaring everyone away?" asked Fred.

"Nothing would make me happier," Sally said. She walked over to the Viking, who was having trouble standing on his rubbery legs. She reached over and yanked off his helmet. A mask came off with it.

"Sasha Kashikova!" she exclaimed.

"Just as we had suspected," Velma said.

"You did? How did you know?" asked Sally.

"We used the clues we found to eliminate all of our suspects but one," Daphne began.

"First we found the Happy Bippy antenna here on the platform," Velma said. "We knew that the Viking dropped it when he was here. And two of our suspects were both wearing Happy Bippys. Sasha was one."

"And I suppose I was the other," Lena Furswich said, walking into the station. "I told the kids how unhappy I was with the way you made the Vikings look."

"That's right," Fred said. "The next thing we found was a piece of paper the Viking had dropped while chasing Shaggy and Scooby." He showed the scrap to Sally.

Sally examined the paper closely. "Why, this looks like part of a drawing of a roller coaster."

"Something that Sasha had shown us," Daphne said. "Your nephew, Gary, also showed us this, remember? But then we found the last clue on the path behind the station. The Viking must have dropped it when he ran out."

Daphne showed Sally the black knob. "Does this look familiar?" she asked.

"Oh, dear, did that come off my remote control unit?" Sally asked, rummaging through her pockets. She took the small black rectangle from her coat. "That's funny.

I'm not missing any pieces."

"And you weren't behind the roller-coaster station before the Viking showed up, either," Daphne said. "You were with us. So only someone else with a remote control unit like yours could have dropped it."

"Someone like Sasha, who used a remote control unit to operate the fantastic fountain in the center of the park," Velma concluded.

"The same remote control unit that stopped the roller coaster," Fred said. "When the Viking raised his sword with one hand, he reached into his cloak with the other. And that's when the Happy Bippy antenna we found fell out."

"Sasha, is all of this true?" Sally asked.

Sasha nodded his head slowly. "Yes, it's true," he announced. "I was angry at you for stealing my idea for the roller coaster. So I decided to get even by making sure no one would ever ride it. I programmed my remote control for the fountain with a microchip that would also operate the roller coaster. I planned to sabotage this Viking-themed monstrosity for as long as it took you to close it down and decide to build the Norwegian Blizzard."

He took the folded-up envelope and drawing out of his pocket and threw it in the air for emphasis.

"And I was this close to getting away with it, too," Sasha continued. "But then those kids and their meddling mutt came along and ruined everything."

Two Happy Sally Land security guards came into the station and led Sasha away.

"The sad thing is that I never even saw Sasha's design," Sally said.

"No wonder," Daphne said, looking at the envelope Sasha had tossed. "He forgot to put a stamp on the envelope when he mailed it."

"Oh, dear," Sally said. "But one good thing did come out of all this. I got to spend some time with Ms. Furswich here. And she convinced me I was wrong to portray Vikings in such a stereotypical way."

"So what are you going to do — turn the Nordic, Nor'easter into the Happy Sally Daisy Coaster?" Gary asked as he came into the station.

"No, in honor of our guests and all they've done for us, I have an even better idea," Sally said with a big smile. "Ladies and gentlemen, I am proud to welcome you aboard the inaugural ride of Happy Sally Land's newest attraction, the largest roller coaster around, the Scooby-Doo Scrambler!"

Scooby's eyes lit up as he grabbed Shaggy and jumped into the front seat.

"Hold on there, Scoob!" Shaggy cried. "I can't go on this thing on a full stomach!"

Happy Sally activated her remote control and sent the roller-coaster car on its way. The gang watched and waved as Shaggy and Scooby made their way up the hill.

"Like, help! Get me off this thing!" called Shaggy.

"Scooby-Dooby-Doo!" shouted Scooby.

Scooby-Doo!

SCOOBY-DOO! ™
MYSTERIES
by James Gelsey

Read them all!

Ruh-roh!
Zoinks!

$3.99 US each!

At bookstores everywhere!